ULTIMATE SCORING MACHINE

I Was Jerry Rice

GORDON KORMAI

HYPERION PAPERBACKS FOR CHILDREN
NEW YORK

Copyright © 1998 by Gordon Korman.

Printed in the United States of America.

First Edition

1 3 5 7 9 10 8 6 4 2

This book is set in 12-point Caslon.

Library of Congress Catalog Card Number: 97-80194
ISBN: 0-7868-1270-2

C o n t e n t s

Warning: No Football

Camp Flagler Bay was a high-action place. The early August sun shone down on furious motion—soccer, relay races, windsurfing, and the Anchor-Defense Flagler Flea-Flicker.

Elliot Rifkin, the quarterback, took his place halfway down the wooden dock that reached out over the sparkling blue water. Behind him, Coleman Galloway crouched into a running back's stance. Elliot waved across the narrow bay to the third member of the Monday Night Football Club. Nick Lighter, the receiver, was positioned behind the antique 1851 anchor in front of the mess hall.

"Hut, hut, *hike!*" barked Elliot.

Coleman sprang up and snatched the handoff in a full sprint. Just when it seemed as if he would run clear off the end of the dock, he put on the brakes. He wheeled and tossed the ball back to Elliot, who reared back and threw.

Some campers playing water polo looked on in wonder as the Anchor-Defense Flagler Flea-Flicker flew high over their game.

"I've got it!" Across the bay, Nick was on the move. He squinted in the sun so as not to lose sight of the perfect spiral. Great throw! The pass was headed right for the old anchor.

Nick made for the mess hall, ready to try a diving catch. Suddenly, a stranger streaked in front of him. With athletic grace, the newcomer dove parallel to the ground. Sure hands picked the ball out of the air just as his body cleared the anchor and hit the grass rolling.

Coleman and Elliot came jogging up, their eyes wide.

"What a catch!" cheered Elliot.

"Who *was* that? Jerry Rice?" panted Coleman.

The mystery receiver picked himself up. He popped a gleaming whistle into his mouth and blew an earsplitting blast that lifted them six inches off the ground. It was Chuck DeSantos, their bunk counselor.

"Have you guys gone crazy?" he bawled. "What are you doing?"

"The Anchor-Defense Flagler Flea-Flicker," Nick explained. "It's a trick football play. The anchor is kind of like a cornerback, covering me on the catch."

"Yeah, well, you could have punctured yourself like a

shish kebab on that 'cornerback'!" the counselor barked.

"I wonder if that would be a penalty under NFL rules," Coleman mused.

Elliot was still marveling over the spectacular catch. "You were awesome, Chuck! You must be on your high school football team!"

For a moment, Chuck's angry face took on a dreamy expression and his gruff voice softened. "I was once—a long time ago—" He shook his head to clear it. "But, guys," he went on in his regular tone, "why are you wasting your energy on this foolishness? Think of all the great stuff you can do here at Camp Flagler Bay. Have you got your swim badges yet? You'll need those for canoeing and waterskiing."

"Actually, we're not too interested in that kind of stuff," Nick admitted. "We're pretty big football fans. NFL, mostly—"

"But we'll watch college, high school, junior high, and even Pee Wee League when the pros aren't playing," added Elliot.

"And we do trick plays," Coleman finished. "You know, like the one you busted up. Otherwise, there's not a whole lot you have to know about us—except that we formed a club to make sure nobody misses *Monday Night Football* on TV."

The counselor regarded his three charges. There was no question about it. These three boys were victims of football fever. And Chuck sure knew about that, all right.

"Listen," he said carefully. "In the next three weeks, you guys are going to have the time of your lives. You'll try new things and make new friends and play all kinds of sports—baseball, soccer, swimming, tennis—"

"And football," added Nick.

Chuck shook his head. "Sorry, guys. We don't play football here at Flagler Bay."

They stared at him in disbelief. To the Monday Night Football Club, no football was like no oxygen.

"Why not?" demanded Coleman.

The counselor shrugged. "For starters, it's summer. It's not really the right time."

"Are you kidding?" protested Nick. "This is the heart of the preseason! That's some of the best stuff all year! You get to watch the rookies fighting tooth and nail to earn a spot on their teams!"

"And you check out the veterans who got traded," put in Elliot. "This is the first glimpse of how they'll fit into the different offenses and defenses."

"Don't forget the Tokyo American Bowl," Coleman reminded them. "San Francisco versus New England on *Monday Night Football*. It's going to be amazing!"

"Forget it, because you're going to miss it," Chuck told them. "There's no television anywhere in the camp. We believe that Flagler Bay is your chance to get away from that kind of stuff—TV, malls, computers, video games. . . ."

Coleman and Elliot looked sideways at Nick, who nodded confidently. The founder of the Monday Night Football Club had his handheld mini-TV carefully hidden in his duffel bag—along with thirty pounds of spare batteries. Nick never took chances when it came to football. He was the ultimate fan. He even had the initials N. F. L., for Nicholas Farrel Lighter.

Elliot faced his counselor. "How can a guy like you not love football? Man, the way you caught the Anchor-Defense Flagler Flea-Flicker—you're a natural! Don't you even play?"

Once again, Chuck's face took on a distant expression. "Once," he admitted. "But that was a long time ago. And a different Chuck DeSantos."

Nick sighed. "Can we at least have our football back?"

The counselor tucked the ball under his arm. "Sure— in three weeks when it's time to go home." He frowned. "Don't look so tragic, guys. You're here to have fun, right?"

"We'd have a lot more fun if we were playing football," Elliot pointed out.

In answer, Chuck popped the whistle into his mouth and blew another brain-scrambling shrill. "There are ten kids in our bunk, and I can't spend the whole day arguing with three of them. The beanbag tournament starts in ten minutes. Be there." And he jogged away.

Coleman was the first to break the stunned silence. "This is a joke, right?"

Nick was very pale. "I don't mind if they feed us bread and water, and the counselors are all ax-murderers, and the cabins are infested with vampire bats. But *please* don't tell me there's no football for three whole weeks."

"Oh, no!" Elliot faced his friends. "Remember when our parents told us this summer was going to be our big chance to 'broaden our horizons'? I'll bet this is what they meant! They did it on purpose!"

"My folks probably picked out the camp that said 'Warning: No Football' on the brochure," moaned Coleman.

"Camp Flagler Bay!" Nick muttered in disgust. "Camp Flag-on-the-Play would be more like it." He folded his arms in front of him. "Well, I don't care what Chuck says. There's no way we're going to miss the Tokyo American Bowl. Even if we have to sneak our mini-TV into the woods and watch the game with a pack of hungry wolves."

"But none of us caught the Anchor-Defense Flagler Flea-Flicker," Coleman reminded them. "That was the rule: Whoever stars in our next trick play gets to wear the Eskimos shirt for the Tokyo American Bowl."

He was talking about the Monday Night Football Club's prized possession—an old football jersey that had been left to Nick by his late grandfather. It was hot and itchy and ugly, but it had a strange and amazing power. Anyone who fell asleep wearing it would somehow trade places with an NFL football hero. Nick, Coleman, and Elliot had each taken a turn playing in the body of a superstar. That was why the trick play was so important. Whoever aced it would be the person chosen to make the switch for the Tokyo American Bowl.

"But how can we try a new play without our football?" Nick mused aloud.

Suddenly, Elliot was smiling.

Coleman was excited. "Look! He's getting a great idea! Let's hear it, Elliot!"

"Beans," said Elliot Rifkin.

2

Broccoli Duty

The beanbag toss championship at Camp Flag-on-the-Play was no small affair. Bragging rights for the whole summer were at stake, along with blue, red, and white prize ribbons for the top three bunks. There were eighteen wooden targets—one for each cabin. The campers took turns throwing while their counselors kept track of point totals.

"Ready for the Bean-Blocker Bean-Crossfire Bean Punt-return?" Nick whispered in the Bunk 8 line.

"Ready," Coleman confirmed. "And Elliot's in position."

Nick snatched a beanbag out of the barrel. "Hut, hut, *hike!*" He bent over and snapped the beanbag between his legs to Coleman. Coleman took three steps forward and punted it with all his might.

The kick sailed past the other teams to where Elliot stood, just beyond the Bunk 18 throwers. As Elliot made the catch, Nick and Coleman dashed out in front of him.

They formed a wedge of blockers for the runback.

It hadn't been easy to come up with a trick play without a football, but the three were quite proud of this plan. Elliot had to return the punt down the alley between the throwers and their targets. The flying beanbags counted as tacklers. If the ball carrier was struck by one, he was officially down and the play was over.

"On your left!" cried Elliot.

Coleman dove forward, knocking down a red polka-dot beanbag from Bunk 11.

Nick blocked two rapid-fire throws from Cabin 6. "Go, man!" he cheered, as Elliot sprang ahead, ducking the beanbag barrage.

Elliot could see Bunk 1—the goal line. His heart leaped. He would be the one to wear the Eskimos shirt for the Tokyo American Bowl. Just a few more yards! He imagined himself at the Tokyo Dome. . . .

Then came an earsplitting whistle blast. Elliot never saw Chuck DeSantos stepping out in front of him.

Wham! There was a blizzard of beans.

Anyone within ten feet was picking them out of shoes, socks, and underwear for the next three days.

The soccer game was tied 2–2 when Coleman reached down and picked up the ball.

"Hey! He can't do that!" cried one of their opponents from Cabin 3.

"Galloway, drop that ball!" bellowed Chuck from the Bunk 8 sidelines.

But for the Monday Night Football Club, the soccer game had ended. In its place, the Soccer-Ball Double-Receiver Jump Bomb had begun.

Coleman dropped back three steps and heaved a long pass. The black-and-white ball sailed clear across the field.

From out of a pack of players leaped Nick and Elliot. As they reached for the catch, both sets of arms got tangled together. The pass bounced first off Nick's head, then Elliot's, and ricocheted past the goalie into the net.

"You were supposed to catch it!" the two receivers screamed into each other's faces.

"What teamwork!" cheered the Bunk 3 counselor. "I've never seen a double header for a goal before! I want you guys to try out for the Flagler Bay All-star soccer team. What do you say?"

"Any chance of getting on the all-star football team?" Nick asked hopefully.

"Football team?" the confused counselor repeated. "We don't have a football team."

"There's no time like the present to start one—" Elliot began.

But he never got to finish his sentence over the angry shrill of Chuck's whistle.

The egg-and-spoon race was the last event before dinner. Elliot's methodical, quick steps had pulled him well ahead of the competition.

"Attaway, Rifkin!" cheered Chuck. "Keep your arm straight!"

Little did he know that he was watching the beginning of the Omelette-Tackle Flying Fumble Runback.

Suddenly, Nick hurled himself in a diving tackle, hitting Elliot just below the knees. Elliot went down; the spoon went spinning off to the left. The egg popped straight up.

Coleman came out of nowhere, catching the egg just before it hit the track. Without breaking stride, he whipped a spoon out of his shirt pocket, placed the egg in it, and started off in the opposite direction. Weaving through the bewildered egg-and-spoon racers, he quick-marched up the course and across the starting line.

"Touchdown!" he bellowed, and spiked the egg. *Splat!*

Furious, Chuck pointed in turn to the Monday Night Football Club members. "You, you, and you! Kitchen duty!"

* * *

"Hold out your plate," Nick instructed. He plopped a mountain of broccoli onto the first tray in the dinner line. "Next!"

"I don't think you're supposed to give so much," put in Coleman, digging into the mashed potatoes.

Nick scooped up another huge portion. "The sooner I get rid of this stuff, the sooner I can breathe again. These gross broccoli fumes are making me sick."

"Don't be such a baby," laughed Elliot, slicing bread. "It's broccoli, not sewer gas."

"Sewer gas would be an improvement," muttered Nick. "I *hate* broccoli!"

Nick and Coleman shoveled and served while Elliot struggled to cut up loaves of bread without losing any fingers. Just as Nick's broccoli supply was nearly gone, a cook appeared and refilled the hot tray.

Nick held his nose against the blast of steam. "Come on! One of you guys do the broccoli for a while."

"Keep your mind off it," Elliot advised. "I've got an idea. You conduct the postgame interview for the Omelette-Tackle Flying Fumble Runback."

"I'll try," wheezed Nick. He held his serving spoon in front of Coleman like a microphone. "Tell the folks at home about your heartbreak at goobering up the trick play."

"I was robbed!" growled Coleman. "I scored that touchdown fair and square!"

"But what about the omelette part?" Nick insisted. "You were supposed to keep the egg and bring it to the mess hall tomorrow morning for breakfast. Instead you busted it, and a squirrel ate it."

"It was kind of an omelette for the squirrel," Coleman argued feebly. "It should have counted."

"Impossible," replied Elliot. "NFL rules. Let's say Jerry Rice fumbles before the goal line and a dog carries the ball in. You think they're going to give Rice six points because it was 'kind of a touchdown for the dog'?"

Angrily, Coleman snatched the spoon "microphone" from Nick. "And now a word from our sponsor," he announced into it. "Folks, have you had a rightful touchdown ripped off? Call Sharkey the Lawyer. He specializes in suing the ref. Don't get even—get rich!"

"Very funny!" Nick wrestled the spoon back. "But we still need a trick play to decide who wears the shirt tomorrow."

The cook burst in again, carrying a tray piled high with bread. "What is this, a talk show? I've got hungry kids here!" He pointed to the cafeteria line. It stretched right out the door and past the 1851 anchor. An impatient buzz filled the mess hall.

"Hurry up and slice that bread!" The man emptied his tray into the bin and stomped back into the kitchen.

Elliot picked up the first fresh-baked loaf. The shape was unusual. It was oval, but it came to point on each end—almost exactly like . . .

A diabolical grin split Elliot's face. "Are you guys thinking what I'm thinking?"

Coleman nodded. "That bread looks just like a football!" he said reverently.

"It's perfect," Nick confirmed. "But what's the play?"

"How about the Bread-Ball Tabletop Mess-Bomb?" suggested Elliot.

"The name says it all," grinned Nick. "Give the signal."

Elliot brandished the bread football quarterback-style. "Hut, hut, *hike*!"

Nick and Coleman ran out from behind the steam trays.

"Don't you dare!" choked Chuck, his mouth filled with Salisbury steak.

The two receivers jumped up onto the center cafeteria table. Side by side, they raced down the long surface, hurdling plates of food. The diners drew back from their thundering heels. Drinks spilled and cutlery shook with every pounding footstep.

Elliot drew back the loaf and threw. The football-shaped bread spiraled out over the two receivers.

At the last second, Coleman lost his nerve and hopped off the table. But Nick extended his arms in front of him. The flying loaf slapped into his hands just before he came crashing down to the floor.

The campers of Flagler Bay rose from their seats in a standing ovation. Elliot dashed out to meet Coleman in a double high five.

Triumphant, Nick sprang back up. He raised the loaf to spike it. Then he remembered Coleman's mistake with the egg. So he took a huge bite of the touchdown "ball," beaming through a blizzard of crumbs.

Nick Lighter was going to Tokyo.

The World's Itchiest Sweater

"You know, you're not being very fair to your bunkmates," Chuck commented.

It was just before lights-out. The Monday Night Football Club sat in the counselor's room in Cabin 8.

"What's so unfair?" asked Nick. "*We're* the ones with another night of kitchen duty."

"Thanks to you, those seven kids were disqualified from every single event today," the counselor said seriously. "All the other campers are wearing the ribbons they won. But not your group. Plus the whole bunk got stuck cleaning up the mess hall after your performance at dinner."

"We were just trying to get in some football," Coleman said in a small voice.

Chuck sighed. "Don't you think it's possible to have too much of a good thing?"

"Not if the good thing is football," Elliot said stoutly.

"I know a guy who had too much football," Chuck told them, "and it almost ruined his life."

"Oh, yeah?" challenged Nick. "Who?"

The counselor looked at them gravely. "Me."

"*You?*" chorused the Monday Night Football Club.

"A year ago, I was the starting tight end on my high school team," Chuck began tragically. "I had the size. I had the moves. I had it all. Big-time colleges were sending scouts to watch me play, and I was only a junior."

"I knew it!" exclaimed Elliot. "The way you caught the Anchor-Defense Flagler Flea-Flicker, you *had* to be a player."

The counselor shook his head sadly. "I had a bad case of football fever. Hour after hour I stared at old game films, searching for holes in the defense. My friends got sick of being told no, I couldn't go out because I had to study the playbook. My girlfriend dumped me. I didn't even notice—*Monday Night Football* was on!"

"So what was the problem?" asked Coleman.

"The problem was I had no life!" Chuck cried. "I used to spend whole weekends in my helmet, bashing my head against the garage door so I wouldn't fumble when I took a big hit."

"I wonder why we never thought of that," mused Nick.

"Don't try it!" The counselor's face was bright red. "It was an aluminum door. I was arrested for disturbing the peace. That's when I knew I had to quit football. I mean, cold turkey. I couldn't play it; I couldn't watch it on TV; I couldn't even think about it."

"But you're awesome!" Elliot protested. "You might make the NFL one day!"

"I've been football-free for over a year now," Chuck said proudly. "It's not too late for you guys to avoid the mistakes I made. Think about that." He opened the door to the bunk area. "Okay, two minutes to lights-out."

The Monday Night Football Club filed out of Chuck's room. Coleman nudged his two friends. Seven pairs of eyes were watching them.

Nick felt he owed his cabinmates an explanation. "Uh—sorry you didn't win any ribbons because of us," he said, shuffling uncomfortably. "We weren't trying to ruin anybody's life. We just had something *really* important we had to take care of—"

"And it's done," Coleman added quickly. "It took all day, but we finally nailed it."

"No problem," yawned LeShawn Marsh, captain of the beanbag team. He didn't sound very sincere.

"We'll be a lot more normal from now on," Elliot promised.

LeShawn rolled over and buried his face in his pillow. There was some not-too-friendly murmuring as the other campers climbed into their bunk beds.

"Day one, and everybody hates us," Coleman whispered mournfully.

"Maybe they're afraid we'll sneeze on them, and they'll catch football fever," snorted Nick.

"What did you guys think of all that?" asked Coleman.

Elliot made a face. "Nobody ever died from liking football. We're still alive, aren't we?" He opened his suitcase and pulled out the Eskimos sweater. "I believe you'll be needing this tomorrow night," he said formally, handing it to Nick.

Nick winced at the thick, scratchy wool against his arm. "It's going to be pretty rough wearing it in the summer," he grimaced. "I don't care how magic it is; it's still the world's itchiest sweater."

"I'll wear it if you don't want to," Elliot volunteered.

"Me, too." Coleman reached for the jersey.

"Get away from me, you vultures!" Nick laughed into his hand. "Go to sleep before you wake everybody up!"

"Too late for that," came a grumble from LeShawn's pillow.

Coleman and Elliot vaulted into their upper bunks. Nick, who was below Coleman, stuffed the treasured brown jersey into his duffel. He jammed the bag into the narrow space between the mattress and the floor and lay back.

Soon the long day of trick plays and whistle blasts caught up with him. As he rolled over into sleep, his left arm dangled off the bed and settled on the wedged duffel. His fingers rested lightly against the sleeve of his grandfather's sweater, which was sticking out of the corner near the zipper.

It wasn't much contact. But it was enough to set off the strange and wonderful effect of the Eskimos jersey. A tiny, glowing football appeared above Nick's dozing form. It began to dance, its path tracing a number through the air: *80.*

"Where—" blurted the sleeping Nick.

The door to the counselor's room opened, and Chuck peered out over his charges. He could have sworn he'd just heard someone talking. His sharp eyes fell on the point of light bouncing over Nick.

"Darn fireflies," he muttered under his breath.

He frowned. Was he crazy, or was that lightning bug shaped exactly like a football?

"Nah!" he whispered as the light winked out. It was those three new kids giving him football on the brain.

It's Raining Money

"—in the world am I?" finished Nick.

Bright sunshine streaked down between the tall buildings.

But it's the middle of the night!

Someone bumped him from behind. A lady on a bicycle brushed by on the right, wheeling him around into a man pushing a cart of souvenir dolls.

The sidewalk was packed! Nick felt like an island in a running river—streams of people rushed past on all sides!

Dazed, he staggered through the crowd and out into the street.

Honk!

A large truck was coming right at him—on the wrong side of the road! Desperately, Nick hurled himself out of its path.

Hold it! I can't jump this far! Nick thought as he sailed through the air.

He landed near the opposite sidewalk. He goggled.

There in front of him stood a genuine celebrity. Nick couldn't believe it. An NFL legend! One of his all-time heroes! What was he doing *here*?

"Look!" he cried aloud. "It's Jerry Rice!"

Then he realized he was pointing into a mirrored window. And in the glass, Jerry Rice was pointing right back out at him.

"Wait a minute—" Nick lowered his arm. So did the all-pro receiver. For the first time, Nick looked down at his own body.

I'm Jerry Rice.

But that was impossible! Only the Eskimos shirt could switch a guy that way. Nick hadn't even put it on.

But here I am. Jerry Rice of the San Francisco 49ers! Three-time Super Bowl champion! The highest scoring receiver in NFL history! I must have touched the jersey somehow—rubbed up against it just enough to start the exchange.

His eyes fell on the strange writing on the window. It looked like Japanese. . . .

Of course! Rice was in Tokyo for the Tokyo American Bowl! It all made sense! Tall buildings, crowded streets, driving on the left side of the road, sunshine—it was night at Camp Flag-on-the-Play, but here in Japan it was the middle of the afternoon!

The switch was on.

Better early than never, he reflected. *Now I've got some time to look around.*

His eyes fell on the building at the corner. Neon lights flashed like in Las Vegas. Loud sounds wafted out to the street—bells, horns, and sirens. On the glittering sign there were English letters along with the Japanese characters: PACHINKO.

Nick stepped inside. It was just about the loudest, most dazzling, high-energy place he'd ever seen—besides a football stadium, of course. Excited people crazily fed coins into *pachinko* machines. These looked a lot like old-style pinball games, but with twenty or thirty little balls in play at the same time.

Nick dug through Rice's pockets and came up with a handful of Japanese change.

He hesitated. Okay, so he looked like Jerry Rice. That didn't give him the right to spend the superstar's money.

But the real Jerry Rice must be in my body right now, he reminded himself. *Mom and Dad shelled out big bucks so I could go to camp.* He grinned. *I'll bet they didn't expect to be feeding and housing Jerry Rice. All things considered, I'm sure number 80 won't mind spotting me a few Japanese yen.*

He found a coin that fit in the slot, and pulled the knob to start his game.

Nick was fascinated. The silver balls were everywhere,

bouncing off bumpers, passing through gates, and spinning pinwheels. He was swept up in the sights and sounds of it.

Suddenly, a twirling red light flashed and a blaring siren filled the pachinko parlor. The other customers broke into applause, and money began to shoot out of the machine.

Thrilled, Nick cupped the best hands in football to catch the raining coins. Soon his wrists sagged under the weight of all that money.

Wow, I've won a fortune!

The next thought that came crashing down on him sucked the air from Rice's lungs.

This was *gambling*! Professional athletes weren't supposed to be mixed up with gambling! Jerry Rice could get in big trouble because of this!

Nick looked around nervously. *At least nobody recognizes me—I mean, recognizes Jerry Rice.*

As if on cue, a teenage boy pointed excitedly. As he spoke in Japanese, Nick picked out the words "American Bowl," "Forty-niners," and "Jerry Rice."

"Jerry Rice. . . . Ah, Jerry Rice. . . . Yes, Jerry Rice. . . ." Now the name was on everyone's lips. And Nick was the center of attention. Coins continued to clink into his hands and onto the floor.

The manager of the pachinko parlor walked up to him and bowed respectfully. "Congratulations, Mr. Rice."

Nick panicked. He dropped his winnings with a clatter and shot out the door. It took all of Rice's talent to weave through the crowded streets. He ducked and cut around the armies of people—

Wham!

The big body he ran into was solid as an oak tree. Its owner was twice the size of anybody on the sidewalks of Tokyo.

This guy must be one of those sumo wrestlers, thought Nick.

The man turned around. It was Dana Stubblefield, the all-pro defensive tackle for the 49ers. "Jerry, where have you been? We leave for practice in five minutes!"

Nick craned his neck to see over Stubblefield's shoulder. He found himself looking at a line of famous faces. The San Francisco 49ers were filing onto their bus bound for the Tokyo Dome.

A Million Percent

The real Jerry Rice tossed and turned in Nick's bunk. These Japanese hotel mattresses were thinner than tracing paper. This one felt like it belonged on a folding cot in a jail cell.

He rolled over and plunged clear off the side of the narrow bed. He sat up and untangled himself from the sheets. What a splitting headache! He struggled to his feet and went to get an aspirin.

But the doorway that Rice stepped through did not lead to the bathroom of his Tokyo hotel room. It was the front entrance to Cabin 8 of Camp Flagler Bay. Rice tumbled down the three wooden stairs and landed in a heap on the grass.

He squinted into the darkness. He *felt* awake, but he had to be still dreaming. This definitely wasn't a five-star hotel. And like many dreams, the world around him made no sense. What was that anchor doing in his room? Yep, he was still sleeping, all right.

Carefully, he climbed up the stairs and crawled back into bed. Darn jet lag, he thought. The long flight and the time difference played havoc with your mind.

Whap! Nick snapped a hard pass out of the air at practice. He tossed the ball away just as quarterback Steve Young launched another bullet.

Whap! This time, Nick had to twist his body and make the catch over his shoulder.

Whap! The throw was so low that his knuckles grazed the AstroTurf as he snatched it up.

Whap! Nick had to jump for this one.

Pow! A trainer smashed him in midair with a huge blocking pad. Nick could feel himself flying backward, and then . . .

Crunch! He landed in a heap. When he opened his eyes, he was amazed to find the ball tightly clenched in the crook of his arm.

Jerry Rice's hands are like football magnets! he thought. *I probably couldn't fumble if I tried.*

Young was shaking his head as he helped Nick to his feet. "Well, Jerry, you're a million percent as usual. In August you're already gearing up to play the Super Bowl."

"Isn't everybody?" asked Nick.

"Haven't you heard?" laughed Young. "Just as a joke,

the offensive line got on the same scale together. Turns out, they weigh almost a ton. Now Coach Mariucci has them on banana diets. The whole group has to lose eighty pounds among them!"

Naturally, the closest attention was focused on the San Francisco rookies. Only the very best would make the team. One big disappointment was Anthony Rockaway, the Niners' top draft choice. Nick knew he was a big college star. But while Nick breezed through the offensive drills, Rockaway missed important blocks and dropped passes.

"Was it this hard when you were breaking into the league?" the rookie asked Nick glumly.

"I don't remember," Nick replied honestly.

"Oh, sure," Rockaway mumbled. "I suppose you expect me to believe that you got here by magic."

Nick just shrugged. The young athlete would never realize how right he really was.

That night, the 49ers were guests at a traditional Japanese dinner of sukiyaki. Nick was nervous because a TV crew was there to film these sports heroes sampling the local cuisine. He didn't want to be caught on camera fumbling with chopsticks or spitting something gross into a potted plant. He was a finicky eater.

Steve Young nudged him. "Remember the sushi from

last night?" he whispered. "Most of us loved it. But a couple of the rookies found out it was raw fish and went home with it in their pockets." He snickered. "You should have smelled the new punter. He's going to have to throw out his suit."

Nick breathed a sigh of relief. Luckily, the real Jerry Rice had eaten *that* meal. Nick couldn't imagine anything worse than raw fish—except maybe broccoli.

The cameramen turned out to be football fans. They had a lot of fun filming the bigger players trying to eat while sitting cross-legged. Some of the three-hundred pound linemen couldn't seem to find space for their tree-trunk thighs and endless legs. The chopsticks looked like toothpicks in their ham-sized fists. Harris Barton's sticks snapped in two in his hand, launching a shrimp dumpling right at Nick's face. Like lightning, Nick reached up and caught the flying morsel in the air.

Wow, he reflected as his teammates burst into laughter and applause. *Jerry Rice doesn't just have the best hands on the football field; he's got the best hands around the dinner table, too.*

His catch made the late news on TV.

After the meal, the team bus took them around the crowded streets back to the hotel. Just as he was about to step through the automatic doors, Nick froze. At the bellhop desk he could see a gleaming golden wheelbarrow piled high with coins. Beside it stood the man from the pachinko parlor!

If that guy gives me a wheelbarrow full of money in front of Coach Mariucci and the whole team, he thought in agony, *Jerry Rice will get in trouble for gambling. He could get suspended or even kicked out of the league!*

Nick knew he could never live with himself if he ruined the career of "NFL's ultimate scoring machine." He looked around desperately. How could he slip into the hotel without the pachinko man seeing him?

His sharp eyes fell on a family of American tourists. A bellboy was loading their suitcases onto a rolling luggage rack. As the uniformed man wheeled the cart through the doors, Nick hopped on and ducked down amid the suitcases and garment bags.

Coach Mariucci looked around in confusion. "Hey, what happened to Jerry?"

Steve Young frowned. "He was here just a minute ago."

The bellboy pushed the cart through the lobby and ushered the tourists into the elevator. Nick felt himself going up.

Suddenly, the hanging bag was pulled aside. Big blue eyes stared at him. It was a little girl of about five or six.

"Daddy, how come there's a man in the middle of our stuff?"

Her father unhooked the bag. "That's not a man," he gaped, "that's Jerry Rice! What are you doing down there, Jerry?"

Embarrassed, Nick picked himself up off the luggage rack. "It's, uh, kind of a Niners tradition," he managed. "Every preseason, a few of us sneak into the hotel."

The man was pop-eyed. "Really?"

"Oh, sure," Nick babbled. "Right now, William Floyd is crawling in through the air-conditioning, and Steve Young is stowed away in a laundry truck."

Luckily, he was able to bluff his way out of the elevator with fast talking and a few autographs. Weak with relief, he let himself into room 1605 using the key in Rice's pocket.

The phone was ringing. It was probably the front desk calling to say, "Sir, we have a wheelbarrow full of yen with your name on it." Oh, no!

He yanked the cord from the wall and the ringing stopped. He shuddered. How long would the pachinko guy follow him around?

Trouble at Camp Flag-on-the-Play, trouble here—Nick felt like he was drowning in trouble.

Keep dog-paddling, he told himself.

Totally Delirious

At exactly 7:00 A.M., Chuck DeSantos poked his head into the cabin and blew three sharp blasts on his whistle.

Jerry Rice leaped up in bed, banging his head on the bottom of the upper bunk.

"Everybody up!" the counselor barked, and retreated back into his room.

"Ohhh," Rice groaned in pain. And when he opened his eyes . . .

"Where's Japan?" he blurted, and instantly clamped a hand over his mouth. That wasn't his voice!

"Asia, stupid," mumbled one of the kids.

Kids?!

He was in a room full of kids—yawning, pillow-fighting, and struggling into clothes. Tall kids, too. They were easily as big as he was. Only—he looked down at his skinny arms and short legs, and felt the jolt of a terrible shock. They weren't big. *He* was *little*!

In a panic, he snatched a pair of mirrored sunglasses

from a nightstand. He stared at his own reflection. He was a *kid*!

"I need to see the doctor *right now!*" he exclaimed over the pounding of his heart.

LeShawn glowered at him. "No way, Nick. You guys messed up all day yesterday and you're going to make up for it today. Don't even think about weaseling out!"

"But I'm sick!" Rice babbled. "I think I have a fever! Something's not right!"

Coleman and Elliot appeared on either side of him.

"Shhh!" whispered Coleman. "Do you want Chuck on our necks?"

Rice frowned at him. "Chuck?" Who was Chuck?

"We need to get off his hit list," Elliot said reasonably. "If we lie low, it'll be easier to sneak away and watch the Tokyo American Bowl."

Rice jumped at the only words that made sense. "I'm supposed to be in that game!"

"And you will be," Coleman assured him. "But we're going to have to be good little campers and pretend to love all their stupid camp things first."

"You've got the wrong guy," Rice insisted. "Listen— I'm a football player—"

"We all are," Elliot interrupted. "But we're stuck at an antifootball camp, with an ex–football addict for a counselor, and we've already lost our ball. We're walking on eggs today—one wrong step and the yolk's on us."

"But—"

The door to the counselor's room burst open, and Chuck was upon them, whistle blaring. "All right, you three! You're back on kitchen duty in two minutes." He glared at Jerry Rice. "And no flying bread this time!"

"Flying bread?" Rice repeated blankly.

"Don't get smart, Lighter!" the counselor snapped.

All through breakfast Rice's mind was a whirlwind of crazy thoughts. He knew all of this had to be some kind of hallucination. But everything felt real—right down to the smell of the hash browns he was spooning out. And those two kids who called him Nick were acting like his best friends.

It must have been the sushi last night! He knew raw fish couldn't be good for you! But the meal had been part of a press conference. Saying no would have made the NFL look bad. So he had eaten spoiled sushi, and now he was seeing things! He was probably lying in a hospital bed in Japan right this minute, totally delirious. He wondered if any of the other 49ers were sick, too.

"I might even miss the Tokyo American Bowl," he muttered under his breath.

"Don't worry," whispered Elliot, who was stacking

strips of bacon on the parade of plates. "An earthquake couldn't keep us from tonight's game."

Tonight? But the kickoff was scheduled for eleven o'clock in the morning. Then he remembered: Tuesday morning in Japan was still Monday night in the United States. This illusion was so real it was scary. That sushi must have been even more spoiled than he thought.

Rice's fever visions didn't end there. After breakfast, he hallucinated a whole volleyball match against Bunk 12. It was hard to believe that the blistering sun in his eyes was a sushi-dream. The court, the teams—the ball whizzing back and forth—it was all so true to life.

Then the ball came floating in his direction. Without thinking, he leaped up in the air and smashed it with all his might. The perfect kill-shot sizzled over the net and hit the ground just inside the line.

"Point for Cabin 8," announced Chuck, the referee.

LeShawn was impressed. "Nice play, Nick."

Some of his bunkmates applauded.

"Thanks," said Rice, pleased.

Now it was his serve. He pounded a rocket that was too hot for Cabin 12 to handle.

"Another point for Bunk 8," enthused Chuck.

"Show 'em how it's done, Nickster!" cheered LeShawn.

Rice smiled. At least his hallucination was turning out to be a pretty good dream.

"Hey, Nick," called Elliot. "You never told us you were a volleyball star."

"Well," Rice replied, "I haven't really played since high school—"

Coleman snorted a laugh right in his face. "High school! Yeah, that's funny!"

The performance was repeated on the baseball diamond. Rice hit a triple and three home runs. He also dominated a track meet and set a new camp record for the hundred meter backstroke in the pool. The competitive spirit of Jerry Rice rose to every new challenge. By the end of the afternoon, Cabin 8 was swimming in prize ribbons.

"Nickster, I am blown away," LeShawn said emotionally. "I thought you were just another flake like—well, like Coleman and Elliot here, no offense to your friends."

"I've been a team player all my career," said Jerry Rice modestly.

"That's exactly why the guys voted you bunk captain," LeShawn went on. "What do you say?"

"It would be an honor," said the top receiver in NFL history. Well, why not? It wasn't *really* happening.

"Three cheers for the captain!" bellowed LeShawn.

Coleman and Elliot didn't join in the hip-hip-hoorays that rang through the cabin.

"I don't like it" was Coleman's opinion. "Since when is Nick Mr. All-Around Camper?"

"It's only an act to get Chuck off our backs," Elliot told him.

"Maybe," Coleman said sulkily. "But couldn't he get them to cut it out with those stupid nicknames? Nickster, Mikester, Davester, Chuckster—I'm going ster-crazy!"

"You're just jealous because Coleman-ster sounds stupid," laughed Elliot.

"Why does Nick have to star at *everything*?" Coleman complained. "He should at least stink at a *couple* of events. You know, out of loyalty to his fellow Monday Night Football Club members so they won't look like total slugs."

"He's not taking any chances for the game tonight," Elliot explained. "You wouldn't either if you were the one trying out the Eskimos sweater."

Chuck appeared in the doorway. "Lighter, Galloway, Rifkin—they're waiting for you in the kitchen."

Elliot looked at him suspiciously. "Aren't you going to blow your whistle?"

The counselor wrapped his burly arms around their shoulders. "I'm proud of you guys. Especially you, Nick.

The kind of effort you showed out there today—that's what camp is all about. I had you three pegged as hopeless football maniacs."

"Excuse me, did you say football?" piped Jerry Rice.

Coleman silenced him with an elbow to the ribs.

Rice winced. For a hallucination, it felt a whole lot like real-life pain.

"I thought you were as football-crazy as I used to be," Chuck told them. "I'm glad you proved me wrong."

"We're glad, too," said Elliot, patting himself on the stomach. For there, hidden in the waistband of his Flagler Bay shorts, was Nick's mini-TV. The *Sport Report* would be previewing tonight's Tokyo American Bowl. And all the kitchen duty in the universe wouldn't keep the Monday Night Football Club from watching it.

Rice On Rice

When Coleman, Elliot, and Jerry Rice reported for kitchen duty at Camp Flag-on-the-Play on Monday night, it was already Tuesday morning in Japan. With the kickoff three hours away, it was time for the Niners' early bus to the Tokyo Dome.

Nick rode in the hotel elevator with Anthony Rockaway. Both of them paced restlessly around the small space until they bumped into each other.

"Sorry," Nick mumbled, embarrassed.

The rookie looked at him with eyes red from lack of sleep. "Man, I know why *I'm* nervous. I'm having the preseason from the black lagoon! If I don't have a big game today, I'm going to get cut from the team. But you— you're a legend! How come *you're* nervous?"

The doors opened on the lobby. Nick flattened himself against the wall of the elevator. "Can you see a gold wheelbarrow full of money out there?"

Rockaway looked hurt. "That's cold! Here I am,

struggling to save my career, and you're joking about wheelbarrows of cash. I don't care about getting rich, Jerry! I just want to make the Forty-niners!"

"No, seriously," Nick insisted. "There's someone chasing me—a Japanese man, short, and he's got a wheelbarrow full of coins."

Rockaway was bug-eyed. "I guess when you're bigtime famous, you attract a lot of crazies. Have you told Coach Mariucci?"

Nick tried to sound casual. "It's no big deal. He's just somebody I have to stay away from. Is he out there?"

Rockaway scanned the lobby. "The coast is clear," he reported.

Nick ran for the bus.

The handheld TV sat half buried in a heaping tray of Rice-A-Roni.

Jerry Rice gawked at the small screen through the broccoli steam. He was watching *himself* being interviewed about the Tokyo American Bowl. When had they taped that? He couldn't remember saying this stuff. That bad sushi must have affected his memory, too!

"Hey, look," chuckled Coleman. "Rice on rice."

"Rice on Rice-A-Roni," Elliot corrected. "They're both the San Francisco treat."

On TV, the reporter was asking about sight-seeing in Tokyo. "What's the most interesting thing you've done in Japan?"

"Well, I haven't won any money, that's for sure!" stammered number 80.

In the camp kitchen, Rice frowned. "What kind of a stupid comment was that?"

Elliot looked at him sternly. "Let's see *you* score more than a hundred sixty NFL touchdowns. Then you can criticize the great Jerry Rice."

Coleman dumped a ladleful of Rice-A-Roni onto the plate of the next camper in line. "Hey, Nick, I can't believe you're not complaining about broccoli duty!"

With his mind on something else, Coleman failed to notice that he'd scooped up the TV with his next spoonful of Rice-A-Roni.

Cabin 8 had reached the front of the line. Chuck DeSantos held out his plate.

"Coleman—" hissed Elliot in horror. "No!"

But it was too late. The TV landed with a clank on the counselor's dish.

"Oops! You got the one with the gristle!" Elliot leaned over the counter and made a grab for the antenna.

Chuck held the tray just out of his grasp. He scowled at the Tokyo Dome on the small screen. "Football," he said, shaking his head sadly. "I'm very disappointed in you three."

"It wasn't Nickster's fault," piped up LeShawn.

The counselor considered this. He faced Jerry Rice. "Nick, did you have anything to do with bringing this TV to the mess hall?"

"No," Rice replied honestly.

Coleman and Elliot exchanged bewildered glances. How could Nick betray the Monday Night Football Club! Nick! The club's founder! The guy with the same initials as the league!

Chuck faced them. "There's going to be a big campfire sing-along and marshmallow roast tonight, but you two don't get to go. You can sit in the cabin and think about all the fun you're missing because of your football fever." He stuck the small TV into his back pocket. "And I'll be holding on to this for the next three weeks."

Oh, no! Twin gasps of agony escaped Coleman and Elliot. It was the absolute worst thing that could have happened! Not only would they miss the Tokyo American Bowl tonight, but the rest of the NFL preseason, too!

Elliot turned anguished eyes on Nick. Surely their friend would be devastated. Instead, he saw Jerry Rice spooning up broccoli as if the world were still okay. Elliot watched in amazement as Rice plucked a big green stalk from the bin and popped it into his mouth.

Stunned, Elliot nudged Coleman, who stared wide-eyed at the sight of their broccoli-hating friend eating his least favorite vegetable. As Coleman leaned forward for a better view, his kitchen duty apron dangled into the warming flame underneath the soup tureen.

"Do you guys smell smoke?" mumbled Rice, still chewing.

"No," Coleman replied, sniffing the air. "Maybe . . . kind of . . ." He looked down. "*I'm on fire!*"

Rice leaped into action. He whipped the burning apron from around Coleman's waist and began to beat it against the top of the serving table. Soon the fire was out. But not before the smoke had wafted into the smoke detector on the ceiling.

The high-pitched, piercing beep of the alarm drowned out the raucous voices in the mess hall. Hands rose to cover ears. Suddenly, the mess hall sprinkler system sprang to life, showering everyone with water.

In the midst of this chaos, Elliot cupped his hands to his mouth and bellowed, "The TV, Chuck—it's not waterproof! *Save the TV!!*"

The counselor jumped up. He'd confiscated this thing; now he was responsible for it. He tucked the handheld set in the crook of his arm.

He began to run, hurdling chairs, tables, and campers like an NFL rusher. His stutter-stepping feet directed him between the sprinkler-heads, keeping the TV dry.

Rice watched him through the spray. "Wow," he breathed. "The kid's got some moves."

There was a lot of laughing and slipping as the drenched campers sloshed behind Chuck out into the late day sun.

"Did you see Chuck?" crowed Coleman. "For a guy who hates football, that was highlight film stuff!"

"Never mind Chuck!" Elliot pulled him aside. "Did you see *Nick*?"

Coleman nodded fervently. "I can't believe he ate broccoli."

Elliot shook his head. "*Nick* didn't eat that broccoli."

"I saw him," said Coleman.

"No, you didn't," Elliot told him. "Because *that isn't Nick*!"

"What?"

"Don't you get it?" Elliot hissed. "First, he's Mr. All-Around Camper. Second, when Chuck takes the TV, he acts like it's no big deal. Third, the broccoli. That's not Nick!"

Coleman frowned. "You think he's crazy?"

"No, I think he's *gone*!" cried Elliot. "He has the

Eskimos shirt, remember? He must have switched!"

"But he hasn't even put it on yet," Coleman protested.

"It must have happened by mistake," Elliot argued. "Maybe he touched it in his sleep last night."

"No wonder we won so many ribbons today!" Coleman exclaimed. "We've got an NFL player in our bunk. I wonder who he is."

Elliot shrugged. "Either a Patriot or a Forty-niner. Take your pick. There are only about a million stars on those teams."

Coleman snuck a quick look at Rice, who was drying Nick's wet hair on his apron. "Do you think he knows what's happening to him?"

"Shhhh. No," Elliot whispered. "And we don't want him to, either. How'd you like to have to explain the Eskimos shirt to the NFL?"

But Elliot needn't have worried. At that moment, Jerry Rice's mind was somewhere else. The all-pro receiver was thinking about Chuck's brilliant "rush" through the sprinklers. It was too bad that all this was a hallucination. Because Chuck DeSantos was the most gifted teenage football player Rice had ever seen.

8

Number Eighty Takes a Penalty

Nick studied himself in the locker room mirror.

Something's not right. . . .

Then he remembered. He reached into the jar of eyeblack and smeared a thick line under each eye. *Number 80's trademark!*

He grinned at his reflection, waved, and posed with a stiff-arm. He couldn't resist performing a Monday Night Football Club commercial.

"Greetings, sports fans. Do you want to wear the same brand of underwear as superstar Jerry Rice?"

A loud chorus of guffaws interrupted him. He wheeled. Coach Mariucci and his teammates were watching him and laughing. But the merriment died when the coach looked at the clock.

"Game time," said Steve Mariucci.

The sound of two hundred voices singing *Ninety-nine Bottles of Beer on the Wall* wafted in through the window of the counselor's room in Bunk 8. The glow from the camp-fire provided just enough light for Coleman and Elliot.

"What if we don't find it?" whined Coleman, digging through Chuck's suitcase. "What if he stashed it some-where else!"

"We'd better pray he didn't," replied Elliot tensely. "The game starts in two minutes. Hey, Chuck has an NFL pocket schedule. Maybe he's not as 'football-free' as he tells people."

"That TV's nowhere!" exclaimed Coleman as they completed the search. "Goodbye, preseason! I'm suing!" In despair, he threw himself backward onto Chuck's bed. As his head hit the pillow, there was a loud clunk. "Ow! Now I'm *double*-suing!" He reached underneath the thin cushion and pulled out—

"The TV!" cheered Elliot.

In half a second, Coleman had turned the set on, and Elliot had located ABC on the small dial.

"Hello, and welcome to Tuesday Morning Football," announced Al Michaels. "Yes, we know it's Monday night in the U.S. But today we're coming to you live from Tokyo, where hard-hitting Japanese business is taking a back seat to hard-hitting American football."

"Turn it down!" Coleman whispered urgently. "We don't want Chuck to catch us!"

"Are you kidding?" scoffed Elliot. "You couldn't hear a bomb blast over that racket."

The sing-along was down to eighty-six bottles of beer on the wall.

"Eating burnt marshmallows and howling at the moon," said Elliot, shaking his head. "Not my idea of a good time."

Coleman was intent on the small screen. "We missed the *Monday Night Football* theme music," he mourned. "But I guess we should be thankful we didn't miss any words."

Elliot nodded. "It's great to be back in the swing of the Monday Night Football Club. Too bad Nick's not here."

"Nick's got it made!" Coleman exclaimed. "For the next three hours, he's an NFL superstar!"

Elliot frowned. "And *after* the three hours?"

Coleman shrugged. "He comes back, same as always."

Elliot pointed out the window at Jerry Rice in Nick's body. "He can't come back. Not unless we can get that guy into the Eskimos shirt."

Coleman panicked. "How are we going to do that? We're banned from the campfire!"

Elliot scratched his chin thoughtfully. "We have to find a place we can get him alone."

"But where?" Coleman demanded. "He isn't budging! He's just sitting there, singing and stuffing his face, and drinking gallons of soda!"

Elliot suddenly stood up. "We'll go to the bathroom."

Coleman stared at him. "I don't have to."

"Yes, you do. And so do I." He gestured out the window at Jerry Rice. "And so will he. That guy has an NFL-size thirst and an eleven-year-old body! All that liquid has got to go somewhere!"

"Hut, hut!"

Nick exploded off the line of scrimmage.

Wham! The New England cornerback bumped him hard. Nick spun off the block, and the defender grabbed him by the shirt.

"Hey!" Nick cried. "That's against the rules!"

The player let go, but now the tight timing pattern was out of sync. Nick flew out on a slant, but it was too late. Quarterback Steve Young had been sacked for a seven yard loss.

"Hey, ref! What about that holding!" bawled Nick.

But the official just signaled for second down.

"Hut!"

This time Nick faked to the outside and blew right past his man. As he sprinted out, Young fired a bullet.

A split second before the pass reached Nick, the linebacker hit him from behind. As he fell forward, the ball bounced off his helmet. Incomplete.

He sprang back up. "Where's the flag, ref? That was pass interference!"

"Third down!" barked the man.

"Oh, come on! He can't tackle me till the ball gets there! It's a penalty!"

Nick kept on complaining. Finally, the disgusted official pulled the flag from his back pocket and threw it to the turf.

"All right, bigmouth. Unsportsmanlike conduct!"

Coach Mariucci yanked Nick off the field. Together they watched the third down play—a long pass dropped by Anthony Rockaway. The rookie was having another rough game.

"Punting team!" called the coach. Then he turned to Nick. "What's the problem, Jerry?"

"Didn't you see?" Nick seethed. "First I got held, then I took a shot before the ball got there!"

"Yeah? So?"

"So there was no penalty call!"

The coach put an arm around his star's shoulder pads. "Look, Jerry. The Patriots rookies are fighting for their jobs. What's the best way for them to impress the coach? By making a play on Jerry Rice."

"But—"

"But nothing!" Mariucci interrupted. "When I see you chewing the ref's ear off, taking a bad flag, I'm asking myself, who's the rookie here? You're a veteran! Not some scared kid in his second game!"

Once I was John Elway and now I'm Jerry Rice, thought Nick. *It's exactly my second game.*

"Look, Jerry," Mariucci said evenly. "There must be a dozen guys in this league who can run like you. Some of them can even catch like you. Do you know why you're great and they're just good?"

Nick stared back blankly.

"Maturity," the coach told him. "Good sense. Patience. Judgment."

Nick took a step back, head spinning. The Eskimos shirt had given him Rice's body. But his maturity?

I guess that doesn't come with the package, he decided.

Being Jerry Rice was going to be a lot harder than he'd thought.

The Most Dangerous Sight in Football

Anthony Rockaway sat miserably on the Niners' bench. The hard-luck rookie was having a conversation with his own hands.

"How could you guys let me down after carrying me so far?" he asked his fingers. "All through high school, through college, you were like glue—everything stuck to you. And now, just when I'm almost at the big time, you couldn't catch a cold!"

Nick gave him a sympathetic slap on the knee pads. He couldn't take his eyes off Drew Bledsoe, the New England quarterback. The Patriots already held a 7–0 lead, and Bledsoe was throwing well. It was only the second quarter, but Nick could see the game slipping away from the 49ers.

Rockaway shook his head. "How do you do it, Jerry? I mean, week after week, year after year. Where do you get that maturity?"

"Believe me—I wish I knew," Nick replied honestly.

What a mess! Here he was, trying to be Jerry Rice, when a few grabs and bumps got him screaming 'No fair!' like a little kid. Meanwhile, Rice's real maturity was twelve thousand miles away at Camp Flag-on-the-Play.

How am I supposed to get mature in the middle of a football game? Nick thought in despair. *I don't even know anybody mature! Coleman—the guy thinks jalapeño peppers should have warning labels from the Surgeon General! And Elliot's a pretty smart guy, but he can have a twenty minute giggle fit over the words "belly button." I don't have any maturity role models!*

The New England drive stalled at the San Francisco forty-two yard line. But instead of punting, Patriots kicker Adam Vinatieri made an impossible fifty-nine-yard field goal that split the uprights perfectly.

The players went berserk, mobbing Vinatieri. The Niners stared in shock, bewildered to find themselves down 10–zip in the blink of an eye. Nick squinted up at the broadcast booth. Even the three *Monday Night Football* commentators were jumping up and down, raving about this rare feat.

A wave of polite applause swept through the audience. Nick's brow furrowed. This was a capacity crowd—forty-five thousand of the biggest football fans in Japan! *This* was their reaction to one of the longest field goals in NFL history? A little bit of clapping?

"I don't get it," Nick told Steve Young. "Back home we'd be lucky if the stadium was still standing after a kick like that! Don't these fans realize what they just saw?"

"Are you kidding?" Young shot back. "The Tokyo Dome is one of the sharpest crowds in the world." He pointed to the grandstand behind them. "Look. Everybody's paying attention, concentrating. They just don't get wild and crazy. That's the culture here. You keep your emotions under control."

And suddenly, Nick knew exactly what he had to do. He would use the *Japanese fans* as his maturity role models. He would play with all of Jerry Rice's ability, but not let Nick Lighter's emotions get in the way.

"Offense on the field!" barked Mariucci.

Nick lined up wide right and waited for the signals from Young.

"Hut!"

Once again, Nick felt the defender's grip on his jersey.

Ignore it, he ordered himself. *Concentrate on your job.*

He bounced off the cornerback, twisting so that the rookie would have to let go. But the speedy runner matched him step for step, badgering him with a swinging arm.

Patience! Nick fought down the urge to shove back.

But all the maturity in the world wasn't going to help if he couldn't get free of this guy.

Rice's body must have read Nick's thoughts. In the blink of an eye, Nick felt himself stop on a dime, fake to the inside, and cut back on an "out" pattern.

Unbelievable! I can go from zero to full speed in a millionth of a second!

By the time the defender realized what was happening, Nick was wide open with a speeding pass slapping into his chest. Three steps later he was going so fast that wind whistled through the bars of his facemask. He could see fear in the eyes of the New England defenders.

I'm the most dangerous sight in football! he reminded himself. *Jerry Rice in the open field!*

Fake left, cut right! With that, the safety was flat on the turf, tackling thin air. Nick opened up his stride and roared into the end zone.

The referee raised his arms. "Touchdown!"

Nick was already planning a celebration that would blow the roof off the Tokyo Dome—screaming, dancing, hurling the ball into the stands—

Then he remembered.

Maturity.

So he placed the football politely on the AstroTurf. The crowd applauded—also politely.

At halftime the Niners were right back in the game, trailing 10–7.

Elliot dropped to the floor of the bathroom stall in the Flagler Bay wash station.

"False alarm," he told Coleman. "It was some kid from Cabin 3."

Coleman sat with his back against the stall door. "I think Nick might be Drew Bledsoe," he said, never taking his eyes from the mini-TV in his lap.

"Really?" Elliot peered excitedly over his shoulder.

Coleman pointed. "See? Bledsoe just scratched his nose! Doesn't Nick's nose itch a lot?"

Elliot rolled his eyes. "Everybody's nose itches. Drew Bledsoe's nose probably itches."

"This is killing me," Coleman complained. "I've got to know which one is Nick. Hey, did Steve Young just wave?"

Elliot squinted at the small screen. "I think he was shooing away that swarm of bugs. No, that's not right. There *are* no bugs in a domed stadium."

"It's just a gravy smear on the TV," said Coleman, scrubbing at it with the sleeve of the Eskimos jersey. "Probably from the Rice-A-Roni."

"Hey, look!" Elliot exclaimed. "Young's going deep. Who's open?"

"Nobody!" cried Coleman. "Rice is double-teamed in the end zone!"

They watched in amazement as number 80 slithered away from both defenders and made a beautiful diving catch.

"Touchdown!" bellowed Al Michaels over the small speaker.

The two Monday Night Football Club members went wild, pounding on the metal walls of the stall and hurling the Eskimos shirt high in the air.

"Rice is *awesome*!" raved Coleman. "They're going to have to build a new wing onto the Hall of Fame just for him!"

"That's his second touchdown tonight!" added Elliot.

"Hello? Is somebody there?" came a third voice.

Coleman and Elliot scrambled up onto the toilet seat so their feet could not be seen.

"What lousy timing!" Coleman whispered angrily. "This jerk's making us miss the replay!"

Elliot hoisted himself up using the top of the stall and snuck a look out into the wash station. "It's Nick!" he hissed. "I mean, the NFL guy in Nick's body."

"I know I heard voices," said Jerry Rice suspiciously.

The football star took a tentative step forward.

Striking Distance

"What are we going to do?" Coleman hissed. "How can we get him into the sweater?"

"I'm thinking," murmured Elliot. "We can't let *him* know that *we* know what he already knows—that he's an NFL—"

"Hey, quit hogging all the foot room," Coleman interrupted. "You're pushing me off the toilet seat."

"Did I ask you to have feet the size of canoes?" Elliot whispered furiously.

"Quick, grab my belt! I'm gonna fa-a-a-all. . . ."

Arms waving frantically, Coleman toppled to the floor of the wash station, yanking Elliot down with him. The stall door burst open.

Jerry Rice jumped back in shock. He relaxed when he recognized his two bunkmates picking themselves up off the cement. "You guys," he began, "you're kind of the camp clowns, right?"

Coleman pointed an accusing finger at Elliot. "It's all

his fault! He wouldn't share the toilet seat!"

Rice laughed and shook his head. "Well, they're waiting for me at the campfire—"

"No!" Elliot cut him off. "Stay!"

Rice frowned. "What for?"

Before he could stop himself, Elliot blurted out, "To get back to your true self!"

The receiver's eyes widened. "You're not part of the illusion," he began slowly. "You're from real life!"

"Right!" Elliot said uncertainly. "Uh—how much do you know about what's going on?"

"I know I'm having hallucinations," Rice began, "and I'm probably in a hospital getting my stomach pumped. Are you my doctor?"

"Exactly!" Elliot replied quickly. He indicated Coleman. "And this is your nurse."

"No fair!" Coleman looked daggers at him. "I'm a doctor, too. I just graduated from medical school last week."

"I'm pretty sure it was the sushi," Rice went on. "My head is all messed up. In my mind, I've gone way back to being a boy at summer camp. And when I talk to you, I see you as two kids from my cabin."

"Uh, yes," Elliot stammered. "I'd better make some notes. Could you spell your last name, please?"

"R-I-C-E—"

Coleman's jaw dropped. "You're *Jerry Rice*?"

He and Elliot exchanged a look of pure delight. This was beyond their wildest dreams! Right now their friend Nick was playing in the Tokyo American Bowl as the greatest touchdown-scoring receiver of all time!

"That's fantastic!" Elliot cheered.

"Fantastic?" Rice repeated. "It's horrible! How'd you like to wake up to discover you're an eleven-year-old kid?"

"Sounds rough," managed Coleman, who woke up eleven every single day.

"You're going to be okay," Elliot assured the future Hall-of-Famer. He held up the Eskimos jersey. "But first you have to put this on."

He and Coleman helped the all-pro receiver shrug into the heavy sweater.

"Ugh!" Rice cringed in discomfort. "Are you sure about this? It's torture!"

"This will keep you warm," Elliot explained.

"I was already warm," Rice complained. "Now I'm burning up!"

"Who's the doctor, you or us?" demanded Coleman.

Elliot felt a pang of guilt at seeing the great Jerry Rice so confused and upset. "Look, Mr. Rice," he pleaded. "I know a lot of things don't make sense right now. But I'm asking you to trust us. If you just hang in there, I guarantee that everything will be back to normal" —he glanced at the small TV and saw that the third quarter was ending—"very, very soon."

New England leap-frogged into the lead on a Curtis Martin touchdown run. San Francisco fought hard to stay within a field goal. But the New England offense was relentless. Early in the fourth quarter, Drew Bledsoe found Terry Glenn with a twenty yard touchdown pass.

Trailing 24–14, the Niners had to dig down deep for the heart to make another run at the Patriots.

Luckily, heart is one thing Jerry Rice has a hundred-year supply of, Nick reminded himself.

The drive didn't start off too well. Anthony Rockaway dropped another pass. Then he missed his block, so running back William Floyd was stopped for no gain. Floyd managed to pick up eight yards on third down. But that made it fourth and two. The punter jogged on, and Nick headed dejectedly to the sidelines. Another wasted series.

All at once, Coach Mariucci flashed him a quick signal. Something in Rice's brain understood instantly. And Nick, thinking with that brain, knew as well. There would be no punt. The Niners would go for it on fourth down. It was a risky call, but this was the perfect time for it. The Patriots would never expect a trick this early in the quarter.

With ten seconds left on the play clock, the punting team rushed off the field. They were replaced by a tight formation of red jerseys—a hard-running, hard-blocking group that specialized in short yardage. The Patriots scrambled to replace their punt-return squad with big, tough defenders.

At first, Nick lined up as a halfback. But as Young called the signals, he split out wide right.

"Hey!" The middle linebacker pointed at him. "Watch Rice!" he bellowed to his teammates.

"Hut!"

Young took the snap and fired a sideways pass. The ball stung as it whapped into Nick's hands.

Where can I go? he thought desperately. *Cut left? Cut right?*

But Rice's legs had their own plan—straight ahead, first down or die trying. Nick took one step and hurled himself forward.

Wham! The tackle rattled every bone in his body. He snapped back like a bowstring but kept his arms locked around the ball.

Out came the measuring sticks. Nick held his breath as the officials stretched out the chain.

"First down, San Francisco!" announced the referee.

The next play was a reverse. Garrison Hearst took the handoff and ran right. Nick darted back to the left. As he snatched the ball from Hearst, he could see that the defense was heading in the wrong direction.

I've got a zillionth of a second to spring loose before the Patriots figure it out!

The thought was barely complete in his mind when Rice's long legs wheeled around the defensive end. He turned the corner like a race car banking a curve in the Indy 500. Dancing to stay in bounds, he leaped over a diving linebacker and cut back into the middle of the field.

Where Jerry Rice is king!

Nick was amazed at how his body always found the best angle to avoid a tackle. It was Nick against the Patriots' secondary—one against four. Then—a fake, a cut, a stiff-arm, and a thirty yard all-out sprint to the end zone.

"Touchdown!" declared the referee.

This time there were some real cheers mixed in with the polite applause.

The extra point made the score 24–21. The Niners were back within striking distance.

I Love You, Man!

Coleman and Elliot tucked Jerry Rice into Nick's bunk in Cabin 8.

"What if my hallucinations get worse?" Rice asked.

Elliot held up the mini-TV. "We've got all your vital signs on this medical monitor." He opened the door to the counselor's room and shoved Coleman in ahead of him. "We'll be right here in this—uh—doctor's office."

No sooner was the door shut than Elliot put the Tokyo American Bowl back on. They sat down on Chuck's bed and watched. The Patriots still led by three at the two minute warning.

"Where do you get the guts to say that medical stuff to the great Jerry Rice?" Coleman said during the commercial.

"It's kinder to let him think he's got a little food poisoning," Elliot reasoned. "He'll go nuts if he finds out all this is real!"

"Here's another question," Coleman went on. "The

game is almost over. Which one of us is going to hit him?"

There was only one way to undo the effect of the Eskimos sweater. If both "switchees" got clobbered at the same instant, they would return to their original bodies. Nick was taking bone-jarring shots every minute in the game. But it was up to Coleman and Elliot to give the same to Jerry Rice.

"We'll decide it the NFL way." Elliot took a nickel from the pocket of his shorts. "With a coin toss. Call it."

Coleman looked scared. "Heads . . . no, tails! No, *heads*!"

The nickel sailed through the air, skittered off the nightstand, and hit the floor spinning on edge. It rolled into a corner, where it slipped through a crack in the floorboards and disappeared.

Elliot looked disgusted. "Got another coin?"

"No way!" Coleman took the flashlight from the outer pocket of Chuck's backpack. He lay down and shone the beam through the crack. He shot back up to his feet. "Yuck! There's spiders down there!"

Elliot got down on his knees and peered through the hole. "I can see the coin," he reported. "It's tails."

Coleman was willing to take his word for it rather than risk a meeting with the spiders. But he did try to negotiate. "What do you say—best two out of three?"

"NFL rules," Elliot said firmly. "The coin toss is final."

"Aw, I have no luck!" Coleman complained. "What can I use to hit him?"

Elliot reached into the closet and came out with a long-handled broom.

"Come on!" Coleman protested. "What am I supposed to tell him? It's not a broom, it's medical equipment? It's a giant thermometer, and I'm going to take his temperature by smashing him over the head?"

A few soft snores wafted in from the next room. Elliot opened the door and peeked out at Rice. "You won't have to tell him anything. He's asleep," he whispered. "That hot, heavy sweater could knock out a tyrannosaurus."

The commercial break was over. Coleman was once again riveted to the small screen. "Get over here!" he hissed. "The Niners are driving!"

Don't let the quiet crowd fool you, Nick told himself.

He looked around. All forty-five thousand spectators concentrated on the field. There was electricity in the air. But it was polite electricity.

With less than a minute to play, these fans know the Niners are in a tough spot!

In the huddle, Steve Young called the play. It was another reverse.

Nick was appalled. "Are you sure? We've got seventy yards to go!"

"They're expecting a pass," Young insisted. "This way, we might catch them napping."

But when Nick snatched the ball from Garrison Hearst, the Patriots were not fooled. Linebackers rushed to cover the end-around. Nick had nowhere to go.

But we're out of time-outs! Nick's mind raced. *If I don't make it to the sidelines, the clock will run down!*

That's when it hit him—an incomplete pass! He could heave the ball out of play to stop the clock. At least that would give San Francisco another chance.

He reared back to throw, and that's when he saw a red jersey streaking through the defense. He squinted at the number. It was Anthony Rockaway!

He hesitated. The rookie had hands like Jell-O. He'd dropped everything so far.

But that's what the preseason is all about! Nick remembered. *To give the new guys a chance to prove themselves! A great catch would wipe out a whole month of mistakes for that poor guy.*

He unloaded the ball with all his might. Rockaway leaped high above the cornerback and pulled in the pass like an all-star.

Energized by triumph, he hit the ground galloping

like a racehorse. One, two, even three tacklers clamped on, and still the rookie staggered forward, dragging them. When he finally went down on the ten yard line, it was with the entire secondary sitting on him.

"Line up!" bellowed Nick, running after the play.

Half a dozen Niners were yelling the same thing. With three seconds left, Young took the snap and threw it into the turf to stop the clock.

Anthony Rockaway was overcome with gratitude. "I love you, man!" he blubbered, enfolding Nick in a bear hug. "You saved my career! I'll never forget this! I'll do anything for you! I'll mow your lawn—"

"Get out of the way!" Nick interrupted, dragging him over to the sidelines. "We've got a field goal to kick!"

Tommy Thompson, the holder, called the signals. "Hut!"

The Patriots blitzed, but kicker Jeff Wilkins got the ball over their reaching arms. It rose toward the goalposts, up, up, and . . .

Coleman stood over the sleeping Rice, the broom raised in both hands.

"Three," whispered Elliot. He was right behind Coleman, one eye on his friend, the other watching the last seconds of the game. "Two—"

And then Jeff Wilkins's kick squeaked just inside the left upright.

"It's good!" cried Al Michaels. "The kick is good!"

"One!" hissed Coleman. He swung the broom down.

Elliot caught it an inch from Rice's nose. He grabbed Coleman and hustled him back to the counselor's room. "Tie game! Nick's going into overtime!"

Coleman watched the replay of the last-second field goal. "Nick is so lucky! Not only does he get to be Jerry Rice—he gets to be Jerry Rice *extra*!"

"Keep the broom handy," Elliot warned. "Overtime is sudden death. And that means sudden broom for Jerry Rice."

Sudden Death

Sudden death.

This was the first Tokyo American Bowl ever to reach overtime. The applause grew louder, and a little less polite.

The next point would win the game. There was nothing polite about sudden death.

Both defenses turned solid as granite. Cornerbacks stuck like glue, and hits registered on the Richter scale. A Patriots field goal attempt bounced off one of the uprights. On the very next series, New England blocked Jeff Wilkins's attempt to win it for San Francisco. Since then, neither offense had made it past midfield.

Coleman was quivering with enthusiasm. "I can't believe it's this exciting, and the season hasn't even started yet! Listen to the hits! You can hear them right through the TV!"

Elliot frowned. "Wait a minute! That's *all* you can hear! The singing—it's stopped!"

There was an urgent knock at the door, and Jerry Rice

let himself into the counselor's room. "The hallucinations, Doc," he said in a worried voice. "They're back."

Elliot pressed the mini-TV against his chest to hide the screen. "That's because you're out of bed."

Rice shook his head. "I was *in* bed when the voices started. I heard this kid from my hallucination—'Where's Nickster?'"

"LeShawn!" Coleman exclaimed in horror.

Rice stared at him. "How do you know LeShawn if he's in *my* hallucination?"

Outside there was the sound of running feet on the steps. The cabin door slammed.

"The bunk's back!" Elliot hissed.

Rice frowned. Something was very wrong here. He snatched the 'medical monitor' from Elliot and found himself staring at the Tokyo American Bowl. "I'm missing the game?"

"No!" choked Coleman. "I mean yes! I mean maybe! I don't know what I mean!"

Then the great receiver saw something that made his eyes bulge. The Niners' offense took the field for one final drive. And *Jerry Rice* was right there with them!

But he was sick! He was *here*!

As number 80 jogged by, he looked right into the camera and bellowed, *"Hi, Coleman and Elliot!"*

It all came crashing down on Jerry Rice. This was no hallucination caused by eating bad sushi! All of this was real! He was someone else—and someone else was *him*!

Suddenly, the door was flung wide, and Chuck strode into the room. At the sight of the three intruders, he popped his whistle into his mouth and blew a gut-vibrating blast. The counselor's eyes narrowed as they settled on the mini-TV in Rice's hands.

"Football," he said sternly. "Again." He reached for the small set.

"Aw, come on, Chuck," wheedled Elliot. "There's only thirty seconds to go in overtime. Please let us watch."

The counselor sighed. "When are you three going to realize there are more important things in the world?" He looked at the screen. "Besides, the Niners are starting from their own six yard line. They'll never make it."

And then number 80 caught a pass in the flat and sprinted for a twenty-five yard gain.

"Way to get out of bounds!" blurted Chuck.

Coleman regarded him oddly. "I thought you hated football."

"Hey," the counselor retorted, "if it wasn't for you guys, I wouldn't even be watching—*holy cow, what a scramble!* Time-out! Time-out!"

Dismayed, Chuck stuck his fist in his mouth. What did he care about this gutsy last-second drive? His football fever was a thing of the past! So what if the Niners were showing incredible courage against all odds?

But as San Francisco lined up for one final play, Chuck couldn't bring himself to look away from the screen. Oh, no! He was supposed to be through with football forever—

"Hut!"

And then he was staring right at it—an open receiver. *"Thro-o-o-ow!!!"* he howled at the top of his lungs.

Steve Young reared back and fired the long bomb. Nick flew down the sidelines, half a step ahead of the cornerback. He could feel the defender's hot, panting breath on the back of his neck. He glanced over his shoulder.

Has Young gone crazy? he thought in horror. *That ball's a mile over my head! Only Superman could catch a pass like that! Superman, or someone who can jump as high as—as high as—*

It exploded in Nick's mind like a hand grenade. *As high as Jerry Rice!*

With a cry of *"Niners!"* he launched himself straight up. At the peak of his leap, he reached above his head and snatched the perfect spiral out of the air.

The cornerback dove to make the tackle. Nick kicked forward like a long-jumper. He hit the turf barely an inch beyond the defender's grasping arms. In a moment of panic, he thought he might fall over backward. But Rice's body righted itself and raced down the sidelines.

As he ran, Nick noticed a new sound in the Tokyo Dome: the roar of forty-five thousand screaming people. The usual quiet politeness had been replaced by a frantic celebration that matched any American stadium.

And why not? They're seeing the NFL at its most exciting—a last-second overtime victory!

Nick streaked for the end zone, waving to the Japanese fans. All at once, his eyes fell on one spectator who was all too familiar. On the sidelines, just past the Patriots' bench, stood the man from the pachinko parlor with his golden wheelbarrow.

The glory of the moment burst like a soap bubble. He had delivered a big win for San Francisco—and now he would deliver big trouble to one of the greatest players of all time. Jerry Rice would be branded a gambler.

And it's all my fault!

He had to avoid the pachinko man at all costs.

He sprinted down the sidelines and crossed the goal line.

"Touchdown!" bellowed the referee.

But Nick kept right on going, straight through the

end zone and into the cement tunnel under the grandstand. Gathering speed, he headed full steam for the exit at the end of the dark hallway. He was so focused on escape that he never saw the janitor wheeling his trolley of garbage cans.

Crash!

"Touchdown!" chorused Coleman, Elliot, Chuck, and Jerry Rice.

"Niners win!" shrieked Coleman.

Elliot slapped him on the shoulder. "Get the broom!"

Coleman snatched up the wooden handle and took aim at Rice. But he wasn't counting on the one-man wild party that was Chuck DeSantos.

"Victory-y-y!" the counselor howled at the top of his lungs. "What a pla-a-a-ay!"

He threw his arms in the air, smacking the broom handle into Coleman's face.

"Ow!" Coleman reeled, staggering into Jerry Rice. Their heads bonked together.

Both fell heavily to the floor of the cabin. When Coleman looked up, the tiny glowing football was dancing over Nick's nose.

"Hey!" cried Coleman.

Dazed, Nick blinked. The Tokyo Dome was replaced

by the itch of the Eskimos sweater. Suddenly he was watching his counselor dancing around the cabin chanting, "Niners! Niners! Niners! . . ."

"But, Chuck," he mumbled in confusion, "you don't like football."

Chuck chortled with glee. "Of course I don't like football—I *love* football! I *live* football! I was an idiot to think I could ever give it up! What excitement! Why, on that last play, I could almost feel myself running down the sidelines in Jerry Rice's body!"

Grinning, Nick winked at his two friends. "Oh, yeah," he agreed. "Me, too."

Steve Young and Anthony Rockaway fished Jerry Rice out of the garbage can on the janitor's cart.

"Let's go, Jerry," Young urged, hustling him out of the tunnel and back onto the field.

"You called me Jerry!" Rice exclaimed. He looked down at his uniform and equipment. "I'm me again!"

Rockaway laughed. "Hurry up. They've named you MVP. Personally, man, I would have crowned you king. But MVP's all they give here."

"Plus there's another special presentation for you," Young added. "Do you know anything about a wheelbarrow?"

Rice frowned. "Like a gardener's?"

"Not exactly—"

The P.A. announcer spoke in Japanese and then gave the English translation. "While visiting our country, Jerry Rice played our traditional game pachinko. Mr. Nakamura from the pachinko parlor will now present him with his winnings."

Rice stared in perplexity as the pachinko man pushed a golden wheelbarrow full of coins in front of him. Mr. Nakamura bowed in the Japanese style and then shook his hand. "Congratulations again, Mr. Rice. You're a difficult man to catch—both on and off the field."

Rice's mind was racing. He'd never even heard of pachinko, let alone played it. As a pro athlete, he made it a habit to stay away from games of chance. No way could he have won this money.

And yet, crazy as it was, it made a lot more sense than the stuff he *did* remember from the last twenty-four hours.

He took the microphone from the pachinko man. "I would like to donate my winnings to the Tokyo Children's Hospital," he announced to the crowd.

The cheers in the Tokyo Dome were the loudest all day.

That NFL Thrill

"What an awesome summer!" Elliot lovingly folded the Eskimos sweater and zipped it into his duffel. "I can't believe we used to call this place Camp Flag-on-the-Play."

It was the last day of camp, and the Monday Night Football Club members were packing their bags for the bus ride home.

"Three weeks of nonstop football," nodded Coleman. "Chuck is the greatest counselor in the history of the world!"

"*After* we got him hooked on football again," Nick put in. "That guy's the biggest football maniac I've ever met. Next to us, I mean." He closed his duffel and frowned. "Hey, my bag's totally empty. Have I forgotten anything?"

"It's all the batteries we used up," Coleman told him. "Ours was the only TV at camp, remember? And Chuck couldn't live if he didn't watch every pregame show, postgame show, *Sport Report*, and the regular-season preview."

Nick nodded. "He had a whole year of football starvation to make up for."

Elliot grinned. "The other cabins must have thought we were nuts. They all gathered around the campfire; we gathered around the TV. And when Chuck started bringing it on nature hikes—"

"I kind of prefer hiking with a TV," said Coleman. "The sound scares away the bears."

Nick snorted. "The only bears we ever saw wore football helmets and hibernated at Soldier Field in Chicago."

The door swung wide and LeShawn strolled into the cabin with his usual greetings. "Nickster! Colester! Elster!"

"Hello-ster," laughed Elliot.

LeShawn exchanged farewell high fives with the Monday Night Football Club. "It was *real*; it was *fun*; but it wasn't *real fun*," he joked. "Just kidding. I'm going to miss you guys."

"Where's Chuckster?" asked Coleman.

"Helping load the suitcases," LeShawn replied. "We're the last to leave. I'm on the bus after yours." He turned to Nick. "Captain, you're a great leader. Although you never quite got it together after the time you won us all those ribbons."

"I wasn't myself that day," Nick admitted honestly.

LeShawn snickered. "Then you must have been Babe Ruth," he said sarcastically.

Surprised, Coleman blurted, "Actually, he was Jerry Rice!"

"Still the smart alecks, huh?" LeShawn shook his head. "Well, see you next year."

The Monday Night Football Club finished packing and headed for the buses.

"I can't wait to get home and start working on some new trick plays," Nick said as they walked. "With all the great football moves Chuck taught us, we're going to be awesome!"

"Hey, guys!" It was Chuck, smiling and waving.

Their counselor and friend tossed their bags into the luggage compartment and shook hands with all three of them.

"Not so hard!" laughed Coleman, wincing under Chuck's crushing grip.

"We'll never forget you," Elliot said honestly.

"Thanks, guys," replied the big counselor. "And not just for a terrific summer. Thanks for reminding me of who I really am—a football player who loves the game."

Nick nodded. "It's a shame it's too late for you to apply to a college with a football program."

Chuck nodded. "Well, there's always next year—"

The camp secretary poked her head out the office window. "There's one last mail call for Bunk 8."

"Thanks." Chuck reached over and accepted two envelopes. He handed the first to Coleman. "Galloway. I think it's another letter from your kid brother."

"Aw, no," Coleman groaned. "Yesterday he sent me a grasshopper from his bug collection. Margaret. I was supposed to release her into the wild." He opened the envelope and poured out five dead ants. "Oh, great."

"No airholes again," commented Elliot.

The other letter was for Chuck. Nick squinted over the counselor's shoulder at the letterhead. "Mississippi Valley State University?" he read. "What do they want?"

Chuck's face went from white to bright red. "They— they're giving me a tryout for their football team!" he stammered.

"That's *fantastic*!" cried Elliot. "But how did they find out how good you are?"

Chuck was overwhelmed. "I got recommended—by their most famous graduate of all time! *Jerry Rice!*"

"Jerry Rice?!" chorused the Monday Night Football Club.

"He said I'm the best prospect he's ever seen," the counselor said in amazement. "It's incredible! Except—I've never met Jerry Rice. And he's definitely never seen me play!"

Nick, Coleman, and Elliot exchanged knowing glances.

"This is the best news in the galaxy!" Nick exclaimed. "I'm positive we'll be watching you in the NFL one day!"

The celebration could have gone on and on. But the bus driver was growing impatient. So the Monday Night Football Club said good-bye to their counselor and found three seats on the bus for the ride home.

Nick sprawled out on the bench behind his two friends. "There's just one thing I don't understand. Sure, Jerry Rice knows Chuck because of the switch. But how did Rice find out that Chuck can play football?"

"It must have been that time on kitchen duty when Coleman's apron caught fire," said Elliot. "Chuck saved our TV from the sprinklers with some killer broken-field running. And Jerry Rice was watching."

"Well, we didn't know it was Jerry Rice at the time," Coleman added. "But we were sure it wasn't you. The guy ate broccoli."

Nick gagged. "Jerry Rice ate broccoli? With *my mouth*?"

Elliot laughed. "Don't worry. It was three weeks ago. It's gone from your stomach by now."

Nick was even more horrified. "Oh, man, it was in my *stomach*, too!"

"It must have affected you," chuckled Coleman. "Your face is pretty green."

"I'll never eat again!" wailed Nick.

"Oh, grow up!" snapped Elliot. "Broccoli's a pretty small price to pay for the privilege of being Jerry Rice."

Nick thought back to the joy of yanking a bullet-pass out of the sky and flying down the field powered by cheers.

"You're right," he agreed. "For that NFL thrill, I'd eat a live toad, warts and all!"

The Official Monday Night Football Club Story of Jerry Rice . . . Simply the Best

There have been so many great players in NFL history, it is hard to call any one of them the best at his position—except for Jerry Rice, that is. He is the best wide receiver ever, holding every major receiving record.

Jerry was born October 13, 1962, in Starkville, Mississippi. At Crawford Moor High, he played basketball and track, in addition to playing football. At Mississippi Valley State, he set 18 NCAA Division II records, and caught more than 100 passes in each of his junior and senior seasons.

Drafted by San Francisco in the first round in 1985, he set a team rookie record with 927 receiving yards. That was just the beginning of an amazing, record-breaking career.

In his thirteen NFL seasons, Rice has set career records for touchdown receptions (1992), total touchdowns (1994), receptions (1995), and receiving yards (1995). He has led the league in receptions twice, and was the first player with four seasons of 100 or more catches. Rice is at his best in big games. After three Super Bowl appearances, he holds career records with 28 receptions, 512 receiving yards, and 7 touchdowns. He was the most valuable player in Super Bowl XXIII.

His Super Bowl record (11 catches and 215 yards) helped the 49ers defeat the Bengals 20-16. (Monday Night Football fans also will note that Rice's 18 touchdowns on Monday nights are the most ever.)

Why is Rice so great? He has speed when he needs it. His height (6'2") is a big advantage. And he has great hands. But most of all, he has an incredible ability to get open. San Francisco quarterbacks know that when Jerry waves his hand, they can just throw the ball. Rice will catch it. But while talent is a big part of his success, few players work harder in the off-season to stay in shape and improve themselves. His running and weight lifting workouts are legendary; football is his job year-round.

When he's not working out, Jerry spends time with his wife, Jackie, and their three kids: Jaqui, 10; Jerry, Jr., 6; and Jada, 1. Jerry also donates his time to local Boys Clubs, the United Negro College Fund, and his own Jerry Rice 127 Foundation.

JERRY RICE

Rice's Best

Through 1996 (Jerry missed much of the 1997 NFL season due to a knee injury):

Eleven Pro Bowls; 1987, 1990 NFL most valuable player; 1993 NFL offensive player of the year; Super Bowl XXIII most valuable player; 1990, 1996 NFL receptions leader; 1995 set NFL single-season record of 1,848 receiving yards; member of NFL's 75th Anniversary All-Time Team.

Jerry Rice is the all-time NFL leader in:
- receptions
- receiving yardage
- total touchdowns
- touchdown receptions

RICE BY THE NUMBERS

	Rec.	Yards	Avg.	TD
1996	108	1,254	11.6	8
Career	1,054	16,415	15.57	165

The Jerry Rice 127 Foundation

I know a lot about scoring touchdowns. After all, I've scored more of them than anyone else in NFL history! But my favorite way to score is to help kids through the Jerry Rice 127 Foundation. (Why 127? When I scored my 127th touchdown, I became the NFL's all-time leader.) My wife, Jackie, and I founded the organization to assist agencies in the Bay Area that help kids and families. We want to help all kids be the best they can be, encourage them to overcome life's problems, and give them hope.

Here are just three of the many organizations that receive aid through our foundation: The March of Dimes funds research aimed at ending birth defects; Big Brothers/Big Sisters provides role models for kids from single-parent families; and the Omega Boys Club in San Francisco helps young people stay in school and stay off the streets.

Whenever you help others, you're scoring one of the biggest touchdowns possible. If you'd like to hear more about the Jerry Rice 127 Foundation, please call (314) 862-1270.

Jerry Rice

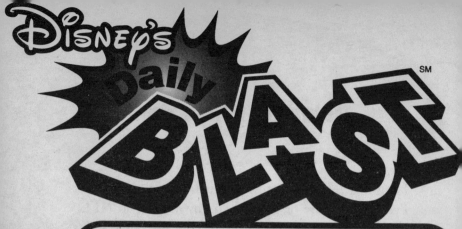

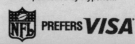